Anonymous

Contract, Specifications and Schedule of Prices of Departmental Buildings, Ottawa City

SALZWASSER
VERLAG

Anonymous

Contract, Specifications and Schedule of Prices of Departmental Buildings, Ottawa City

Reprint of the original, first published in 1859.

1st Edition 2022 | ISBN: 978-3-37512-210-2

Verlag (Publisher): Salzwasser Verlag GmbH, Zeilweg 44, 60439 Frankfurt, Deutschland
Vertretungsberechtigt (Authorized to represent): E. Roepke, Zeilweg 44, 60439 Frankfurt, Deutschland
Druck (Print): Books on Demand GmbH, In de Tarpen 42, 22848 Norderstedt, Deutschland

CONTRACT, SPECIFICATIONS

AND

SCHEDULE OF PRICES

OF

DEPARTMENTAL BUILDINGS,

Ottawa City, C. W.

QUEBEC:

PRINTED BY STEWART DERBISHIRE & GEORGE DESBARATS,

Printer to the Queen's Most Excellent Majesty.

1859.

CONTRACT, &c.

OF

DEPARMENTAL BUILDINGS,

OTTAWA CITY, C. W.

𝕿𝖍𝖎𝖘 𝕴𝖓𝖉𝖊𝖓𝖙𝖚𝖗𝖊 made this Seventh day of December, in the year of Our Lord one thousand eight hundred and fifty-nine, between RALPH JONES, of the Town of Port Hope, in the County of Durham, Esquire, EDWARD HAYCOCK, of the same place, Esquire, and THOMAS C. CLARK, of the same place, Civil Engineer, carrying on business as Contractors for building under the firm of " Jones, Haycock and Company," and hereinafter throughout designated as " The Contractors," of the first part, and HER MAJESTY QUEEN VICTORIA, represented herein by the Honorable THE COMMISSIONER OF PUBLIC WORKS, of the Province of Canada hereinafter throughout designated as " The Commissioner," of the second part.

WHEREAS the Government of the Province of Canada have, in pursuance of an Act of Parliament of the said Province, and of certain Resolutions to that effect of the Legislature of the said Province, determined to erect buildings at the City of Ottawa hereinafter mentioned for the use, occupation and accommodation of the Legislature and of the several Public Departments, of Her Majesty's Civil and Militia Service of Canada ; And Whereas for the purpose of carrying the same into effect, Plans and Specifications have been prepared for buildings, for the use and accommodation of the several Public Departments, of Her Majesty's Civil and Militia Service of Canada, and of the Officers and Servants thereof, (and which buildings are hereinafter throughout designated as " The Departmental Buildings,") by Messrs. Stent and Laver, the Architects thereof ; And Whereas the Contractors have agreed to and with Her Majesty the Queen to erect, build and complete the several buildings, and to supply all proper and requisite materials therefor, upon the terms and subject to the conditions, stipulations and agreements hereinafter contained—Now this Indenture witnesseth, That in consideration of the sum of

1*

CONTRACT.

Two Hundred and Seventy-eight Thousand Eight Hundred and Ten Dollars of lawful money of Canada, to be paid to the Contractors, their Executors, Administrators and Assigns, by Her Majesty, Her Heirs or Successors, in manner hereinafter mentioned—They, the Contractors, do and each and every of them, doth hereby for themselves and himself, and for the Heirs, Executors, Administrators and Assigns of themselves and himself respectively, jointly, and severally covenant, promise and agree, to and with Her Majesty the Queen, Her Heirs and Successors in manner following, that is to say :

1. They, the Contractors, shall well truly and faithfully build, erect, construct, complete, and finish in the best and most workmanlike manner, in every respect and of the best materials of their several kinds, including the fireproofing of the whole thereof, and to the satisfaction of the Commissioner, the Departmental Buildings to be built, erected, and placed in and upon such portion or portions of the land, known as " The Barrack Hill," in the City of Ottawa, as may be pointed out to the Contractors for that purpose, and according to the Plans and Specifications thereof respectively, and which Plans and Specifications as to the Departmental Buildings are signed by Messrs. Stent and Laver, the Architects of the said last mentioned buildings, and by the Contractors, and the Plans whereof so signed, are deposited of record in the Department of Public Works, and the Specifications whereof so signed are hereunto annexed marked A, and a Specification of additional work to be done in making Fire-proof the Departmental Buildings, also signed and hereunto annexed, marked B, and which said papers A and B are respectively also to be construed and read as part hereof, and as if embodied in and forming a part of this Contract, and further that the Contractors in the erection, construction, and completion of the said buildings respectively, and in every matter or thing connected therewith, or incident or relative thereto, shall be guided and bound, by such further working detailed Plans and Instructions as may, from time to time, be furnished and supplied to them by the Architects in charge.

2. The Contractors shall and will, preparatory to or in course of erection of the works embraced in this Contract, make and complete all necessary excavations, and shall find and supply all necessary and proper scaffolding, materials, tools, implements and plant of whatsoever kind or description, for the erection, construction and completion of the said works, and every part thereof, and shall also find and work and temporarily place, such examples

CONTRACT.

of the work or moulds or patterns thereof, in experiment to test
the style or effect, and from time to time, shall alter, vary or
renew the same, as the Architects in charge or the Clerk of Works
may require, and, further that all materials—the said work,
shall, before being used, be inspected and approved of by the
Architects in charge, or by the Clerk of Works acting under their
orders, and any materials disapproved of, and rejected by the said
Architects or the Clerk of Works, as aforesaid, shall not be used
in the works, and if not removed by the Contractors, when directed by the Architects or Clerk of Works aforesaid, then the
same shall be removed by the Architects or Clerk of Works
aforesaid, to such place as they may deem proper, at the cost,
charge and risk of the Contractors; but any such inspection, and
any approval of materials, shall not in any wise subject or make
liable Her Majesty to pay the Contractors, for the said materials
so approved or any portion thereof, unless employed or used in the
said works, nor prevent the rejection afterwards, of any portion
thereof which may prove or turn out at any time, before the final
completion of this contract, to be unsound or unfit or improper,
to be used in the works, nor shall such inspection be considered
as a waiver of objection to the work, or any part thereof, on the
account of unsoundness or imperfection of the materials used.

3. The Contractors shall forthwith immediately commence the
works embraced in this contract, and shall proceed with the same
from time to time, and the same respectively and every part and
parcel thereof shall be fully, thoroughly, and entirely completed in
their several particulars, and given up, under final certificate, and
to the satisfaction in all respects of the Commissioner and of the
Architects in charge thereof, on or before the First day of February,
which will be in the year of Our Lord, one thousand eight hundred
and sixty-two, time being of the essence of the contract, and
further that in failure of completion as aforesaid, at the period
hereinbefore specially limited for the completion thereof, the
Contractors shall forfeit all right, claim or demand to the sum of
money or percentage hereinafter agreed to be retained by the
Commissioner, and any and every part thereof, as also to any
moneys whatever, which may be at the time of the failure of the
completion as aforesaid, due or owing to the Contractors, and that
the Contractors shall also pay or cause to be paid, to Her Majesty,
as liquidated damages, and not by way of fine or penalty, the sum
of two hundred dollars for each and every week, and the fractional
part of such sum for every part of a week for which the works,
within this contract or any portion thereof, may remain incomplete,

or for which the certificate of the Architects in charge of the completion of the said works, or any part thereof may be withheld, and the Commissioner may deduct and retain in his hands, such sums as may become due, as liquidated damages from any sum of money then due or payable, or to fall or become due or payable thereafter to the Contractors.

4. That in case of inclement weather occurring, whether during the progress of the works, which in the opinion of the Commissioner or Architects in charge of the same, respectively, may be detrimental thereto, or during the period when the works may be suspended, in whole or in part by the Commissioner, or the Architects in charge of the said works, respectively, for the winter season or otherwise, such precautions shall be taken by the Contractors at their own outlay and cost, and without any charge or claim in respect thereof, as may in that view be directed by the Commissioner or Architects in charge, and that any such direction of the Commissioner or the Architects in charge, shall not be taken or held in any manner whatsoever, to involve Her Majesty in any responsibility in regard to the preservation of the work, and further that if the Contractors fail in such precautions, the same may be adopted by the Commissioner or the Architects in charge, and the Commissioner may deduct and retain in his hands, out of the percentage hereinafter mentioned, or out of any moneys which might otherwise at any time become or fall due to the Contractors, all such sums of money, damages and expenses as shall have been incurred, defrayed or expended in the adoption of such precaution as aforesaid.

5. The care of the works under this contract and of every part thereof, and of the materials, tools, implements and every thing belonging or appertaining thereto, shall be entirely at the charge of the Contractors, and they shall be liable and responsible for all loss, damage, detriment or injury that may arise or be sustained during the progress of the works, and until the said buildings shall have been certified by the Architects in charge as complete, and have been delivered to and received by the Commissioner on the part of Her Majesty, and further that in the event of any loss, damage, detriment or injury, the property so lost, damaged, deteriorated or injured shall be replaced, reconstructed, restored, renewed or amended as the case may be, to the satisfaction of the Commissioner or of the Architects in charge, and further that if the Contractors fail in the replacing, reconstruction, restoration, renewal or amendment of such lost, damaged, deteriorated or injured property, the same may be so replaced,

reconstructed, restored, renewed, or amended by the Commissioner, and the Commissioner may deduct and retain in his hands, out of the percentage hereinafter mentioned, or out of any moneys which may otherwise at any time become or fall due to the Contractors, all such sums of money and expenses as shall have been so incurred, defrayed, or expended by the Commissioner for such purpose, or the Commissioner may recover the same, from the Contractors as in the next succeeding clause mentioned.

6. On failure of the Contractors to complete the works herein contracted for, at the period of time hereinbefore mentioned, the Contractors shall be liable for, and shall pay or cause to be paid to Her Majesty, all percentage, salaries or wages, which shall become due to the Architects in charge, Clerk of Works, or subordinate person or persons superintending the work on behalf of the Commissioner, from the period so hereinbefore named for completion of the works, up to and until the said works, shall actually be completed and received, and the Commissioner may deduct and retain in his hands out of the percentage hereinafter mentioned, or out of any moneys which may otherwise at any time become or fall due to the Contractors, all such sums of money and expenses, as shall have been so incurred, defrayed or expended, by the Commissioner for such purpose, or the Commissioner may recover the same from the Contractors, on, an action in the name of Her Majesty, as moneys paid for and on account of the Contractors.

7. If it shall, at any time, appear to the Commissioner, that the establishment or the rate of progress at, in and upon the said works or any of them, or of any work or matter incident to the same, or in any way connected therewith, are not satisfactory, or such as to ensure the completion of the same, within the time hereinbefore mentioned, or on failure or breach by the Contractors, of any matter or thing herein contained, on the part of the Contractors to be done or performed, or if the Contractors shall, at any time or times, neglect or refuse to carry on this contract or any part of it, or to supply requisite and proper scaffoldings, tools, implements, or plant or materials, or are unable to carry on the same, then and in any of such cases, the Commissioner may forthwith, after having given three days' notice to the Contractors, of his intention so to do, and without any process or suit at Law, or other legal proceeding of any kind whatever, or without its being necessary to place the Contractors *en demeure*, either absolutely take the works, or any part thereof, out of the hands of the Contractors, and relet the same without the necessity of previous advertisement, or employ additional workmen, and provide mate-

rials, tools, implements, and all other things requisite for the completion and performance of the contract, at the expense of the Contractors ; and the Contractors shall, in either case, be liable for all damages, and extra costs and expenditure, which may be incurred by reason thereof ; and if such damages, extra costs and expenditure, exceed in the whole the said sum of two hundred and seventy-eight thousand eight hundred and ten dollars, then Her Majesty may recover of and from the Contractors, the balance or excess over and beyond the said sum of two hundred and seventy-eight thousand eight hundred and ten dollars.

8. If any overseer, mechanic, or workman, employed on or about the works or any portion, be incompetent to perform the work or duties required of him, or give just cause of complaint, the Contractors shall immediately, upon the application of the Architects or Clerk of Works, dismiss such person or persons forthwith from the works, and he shall not be employed again thereon, without the written consent of the Architects or Clerk of Works, and should the Contractors continue to employ such overseer, mechanic or workman, the Contractors shall pay to Her Majesty, Her Heirs and Successors, the sum of Twenty Dollars, as liquidated damages, and not of fine or penalty, for each and every day during which such overseer, mechanic or workman shall be employed, on the works after such application for his dismissal as aforesaid, and the Commissioner shall have the same power of retaining such sums, as may become due to Her Majesty under this clause, or of enforcing payment thereof as are given and expressed in the sixth clause of this contract.

9. That whenever and so often as it may be necessary for the Contractors, to co-operate with any person contracting for supplying or placing the apparatus for heating the buildings, the Contractors shall diligently, and under the directions of the Architects in charge or the Clerk of Works, perform all such works as shall be requisite, or proper on the part of the Contractors for building in, securing, and placing in proper position the flues or other apparatus, required for heating in a proper and secure mode, and to prevent the possibility of accident by fire therefrom, without any extra charge therefor, and shall be bound in all things, to conform to the direction of the Commissioner, touching such work.

10. That when any discrepancy exists between the dimensions, as indicated by the scale of any drawing, and the dimensions marked in figures on the plans or on any drawings which may be from time to time supplied by the Architects, to the Contractors for the purpose of working therefrom, the figures are in all cases

to be considered correct, and if there should be any discrepancy between the figures or dimensions, or the form of the construction, or the material as indicated by the plans or drawings, and the dimensions and description given in the specifications, the directions of the Commissioner or the Architect in charge, shall be adopted in reference to such discrepancy, and shall be binding and conclusive on the Contractors.

11. Whenever neither the plans, drawings or the specifications, contain any notice of minor parts, the intention to include which is nevertheless clearly to be inferred, and minor and detailed parts are common, usual and proper in workmanship of the same or a similar character, and which are obviously necessary, to the due completion or stability of the work, all such parts and the necessary materials therefor, or the necessary tools and implements, for working up the same are to be found, completed, provided and fixed by the Contractors, and are to be considered as included in this contract, and not as extra work, it being the intention of this covenant, that all such work of every kind as may be necessary, for completely finishing the works proposed in the best and most workmanlike manner, and for the rectification of any failure from whatever cause arising, and the well maintaining, sustaining, and supporting the whole of the works, as well as any and whatever change, alteration and addition, that may be made thereon, so that the whole may remain sound and firm, are implied in the plans, specifications and drawings heretofore mentioned, although the same are not therein specifically expressed.

12. That the Contractors shall not in any way, directly or indirectly sell, dispose of, relet, assign, transfer, or sublet to any person or persons whomsoever, either entirely or partially, and jointly with himself, or in any other manner or way howsoever, this contract or any part thereof, or any portion of the work embraced herein, or to be performed hereunder, or which without being distinctly and specially mentioned herein, may yet be rendered necessary, for the full and proper completion of the contract.

13. That any notice or other paper connected with this contract, which may be required or desirable on the part of Her Majesty, may be served on the Contractors, either at his or their usual domicile, or at his or their usual place of business, at the City of Ottawa, by being left at the Post Office, and any notice or other paper so addressed, and left at the Post Office, shall to all intents and purposes be considered legally served. And the Contractors and Her Majesty the Queen do, and each of them doth, hereby

further, mutually covenant, promise and agree, the one with the other of them, the Contractors, for themselves, their heirs, executors, administrators and assigns, and Her Majesty, for Herself, Her Heirs and Successors, in manner following, that is to say :

1. That payment of any sums of money which may be made to the Contractors by Her Majesty under this contract, will be so made according to the provisions of the Act of Parliament of this Province, passed in the 2nd Session of the 22nd Vic. chap. 3, sec. 18 ; and within ten days after an estimate of the Architects in charge, shall have been received by the Commissioner, specifying the amount of work done, according to the terms and conditions of this contract, during the month then ending ; but nevertheless the Commissioner, on behalf of Her Majesty, shall withhold from the Contractors, and retain ten per cent. out of the amount of the estimates, until the perfect completion and acceptance by the Commissioner of the work, which ten per cent. so withheld and retained, shall be paid with the last instalment, unless retained by the Commissioner as hereinbefore mentioned within ten days after the Architect in charge, shall have delivered to the Commissioner, his final estimate of the work performed, and the materials furnished, in virtue of this contract, with detailed measurements, weights and other quantities, and his or their certificate of the work having been fully completed and finished, if the Commissioner shall so soon have accepted and approved of the work ; and that in forming their final estimate, the Architects in charge shall not be bound or governed by the preceding monthly estimates, which shall be considered and taken as merely approximate. And it is expressly declared that the monthly payments, to be made to the Contractors as hereinbefore mentioned, shall be made upon the basis of the schedule of prices, hereunto annexed marked C, to be nevertheless regulated, determined and applied in all cases whatever, by the Commissioner or the Architects in charge, and upon none other basis or scale, and further that the presentation of the monthly estimate of the Architects in charge, shall not of itself entitle the Contractors, to demand payment of the amount to be paid as hereinbefore mentioned.

2. That it shall be in the power of the Commissioner, on behalf of Her Majesty, to make payments or advances on materials, implements, vessels, or tools of any description procured for the works, or used or intended to be used about the same, in such cases and upon such terms and conditions, as to the said Commissioner may seem proper, and that whenever any advance or payment shall be made to the Contractors upon any tools, implements or

materials of any description, the tools, implements or materials, upon which such advance or payment shall be made, shall thenceforward be vested in, and held as collateral security by Her Majesty, Her Heirs and Successors, for the due fulfilment by the Contractors of the present contract, it being however well understood that all such tools, implements or materials of any kind, are to remain at the risk of the Contractors, who shall be responsible for the same, until finally used and accepted as part of the work by the Commissioner ; but the Contractors shall not exercise any act of ownership or control whatever over any tools, implements or materials, upon which any advance or payment has been so made, without the permission in writing of the Commissioner.

3. In this contract the words " Her Majesty " or " Her Majesty the Queen," shall mean Her Majesty, Her Heirs and Successors.

The words " The Commissioner " shall mean The Commissioner of Public Works, of the Province of Canada for the time being.

The words " The Contractors " shall mean the hereinbefore mentioned Ralph Jones, Edward Haycock and Thomas C. Clarke, carrying on business as Contractors for building, under the firm of Jones, Haycock and Company, and the Heirs, Executors, Administrators and Assigns of them and each and every of them, jointly and severally.

The words " The Departmental Buildings " shall mean the buildings and erections as designed by the Architects thereof, according to the plans thereof hereinbefore mentioned, and the specifications thereof hereunto annexed marked A, and the specification for fireproofing hereunto annexed marked B, and to be erected for the use, occupation and accommodation of the several Public Departments of Her Majesty's Civil and Militia Service of Canada, and of the Officers and Servants thereof respectively.

The words " Architects " or " Architects in charge " shall mean Messrs. Stent and Laver, of the City of Ottawa, Architects, or such other person or persons, as may be appointed by the Commissioner to act as Architects in the room and stead of the said Messrs. Stent and Laver.

The construction of the words given in this clause shall not control any more extended construction, which may be given to any of such words throughout this contract.

4. That if any change, alteration or addition, either in the position or details of the works embraced in this contract, or in any of the materials therefor, shall be required by the Commissioner, the Contractors will make such change, alteration or addi-

tion, and if such change, alteration or addition shall entail extra expense on the Contractors, either in labour or materials, the same shall be allowed to the Contractors, or should it be a saving to the Contractors in either labour or materials, the same shall be deducted from the amount of this contract; but no such change, alteration or addition, whatever may be the extent or quality thereof, or at whatever time the same may be acquired to be made pending this contract, shall in anywise have the effect of suspending, superseding, annulling or rescinding this contract, which shall continue to subsist, notwithstanding any such change, alteration or addition; and every such change, alteration or addition, shall be performed, and made by the Contractors, under and subject to the conditions, stipulations, and covenants herein expressed, as if such change, alteration or addition had been expressed, and specified in the terms of this contract; but no change, alteration or addition as aforesaid whatever, and no extra work whatever, shall be done without the written authority of the Commissioner, given prior to the execution of the work, nor will any allowance or payment whatever, be made for the same in case it should be done without such authority.

In Witness whereof, the said The Contractors hath hereunto set their hands and affixed their seals, and the Honorable John Rose, Commissioner of Public Works of the Province of Canada, for the time being, acting herein on behalf of Her Majesty, hath set his hand and seal the day and year first above written.

(Signed,) { RALPH JONES,
EDWARD HAYCOCK,
THOS. C. CLARK,
JOHN ROSE, Commissioner.

Signed, Sealed and Delivered, (by the w.thin named Ralph Jones, and by the Honorable John Rose, the several interlineations, additions and erasures throughout this Deed, having been made prior to the delivery thereof, and being initialed in the margin thereof by me the attesting witness)

In presence of,

(Signed,) H. BERNARD, Chief Clerk,
Office of Attorney General, U. C.

And by the within named,

EDWARD HAYCOCK

AND

THOS. C. CLARK,

In the presence of,

(Signed,) J. J. BURROWES, County Attorney,
United Counties of N. & D.

v

SPECIFICATION

Of the several Works to be done in erecting and completely finishing two detached Buildings, on the Barrack Hill, in the City of Ottawa, (C. W.) known as DEPARTMENTAL BUILDINGS, for THE HONORABLE THE COMMISSIONER OF PUBLIC WORKS, and according to Drawings prepared by MESSRS. STENT & LAVER, *Architects*.

~~~~~~~~~~~~~~~~~~~~~~

All the Works are to be executed in the best and most workmanlike manner, and all the materials are to be unexceptionable in quality, and both workmanship and materials, must be prepared and executed, to the entire satisfaction of the Commissioner and Architects.

~~~~~~~~~~~~~~~~~~~~~~

Excavator.

Excavation. The whole of the two sites which is required for rooms on the basements and the areas, is to be excavated of sufficient size and depth to build them, as shewn on the plans, the surface of the spaces so excavated being left at a perfect level to receive the masonry. Dig one foot below the said level, trenches to receive the various walls forming the rooms, and of sufficient width for the footings, or in every case two feet wider than the thickness of the walls themselves. Excavate on the remaining portion of the two sites for all foundation walls, at an uniform depth of four feet, or starting with that depth at the lowest point, and in every case to be two feet wider than the thickness of the walls themselves, in order to receive the footings, and to be of an uniform level throughout at the bottom of the trenches, subject only to breaks in the heights or steps, to meet the unlevel nature of the ground, as shewn by the Section and Block Plan.

Levelling. The general surface of the ground enclosed by the buildings themselves, and not required for rooms, is to be brought to a tolerably even surface, and to be levelled to at least 3 feet below the ground floor joists,—to admit of ample ventilation.

NOTE.—Places of deposit for the surplus material may be obtained near the building, for road making purposes, (see Streets Commissioner.)

Removal of rubbish.

Perform also all excavation for drains, areas, ventilating funnels, water pipes, or otherwise, required to carry on the works ; and remove from the buildings and grounds adjacent thereto, all excavated soil, rubbish, stone, or other material to some convenient place of deposit on the Barrack Hill. The stone which may be of good quality, may be retained for use in the building. So much of the soil rubbish, chippings, spaults, &c., as may be directed to be used round about the walls, to be deposited in such forms as may be directed. The whole buildings and site to be left free from all rubbish or useless material of any kind, at the completion of the works.

Excavation for towers.

The excavation for the principal Tower to be lower than the ordinary walls of the building, and to be of the depth shewn by the section.

Filling in.

As soon as the walls are built up to the ground level, the spaces all round are to be filled in and well rammed, the same also to the trenches for drains, pipes, and otherwise, throughout. The depth of excavation for drains to be 4 feet at the shallowest part.

Removal of water.

Immediate provision to be made for the thorough and complete drainage of every part of the foundations of each block of buildings, and the same is to be maintained until the works are completed, and the permanent system of drainage is in successful operation.

Mason.

Kind of stone for foundation.

All the stones used in the building, except otherwise described, are to be the blue lime stone of the district, carefully selected. The whole of the foundation, walls, and walls of the basement, (except otherwise shewn on plans,) are to be built of rough rubble masonry of the height and thickness shewn on the plans and sections, and in every case throughout each building are to have footings of two courses, each six inches deep, and not less than four inches projection, care being taken to construct the footings of even flat stones of the largest description. Holes to be left in the walls below the floor, and cast-iron ventilating bricks built in to allow for the free circulation of air. The iron bricks to be supplied by the ironfounder.

Stone walling and tar and gravel.

Lay over whole of the walls, immediately below the ground-line, on a surface of brick laid flat, and built nearly to the external face of the walls, set in cement, a coating of felt, covered with tar and gravel, not less than half an inch thick, the same to remain till it is perfectly hard previously to being built upon, flags of sandstone for similar use, to be built over the walls of the towers, also set in cement. The upper external walls are to be built on an average of 21 inches thick, exclusive of all projections, to be in rough rubble masonry, finished on the external surface similar to the specimens erected on the grounds for contractors guidance, having horizontal beds and vertical joints, hammered only, and not tooldressed, the pointing to be with an indented joint in blue mortar, prepared with smiths blowings and other materials as will be directed, no joint to exceed one quarter of an inch in thickness. Such specimens are to remain until the completion of the mason's contract, and to be the standard at which all his work will require to be done. The random coursed work for ordinary walls; the rubble work in the positions shewn on the elevations. The joints to be raked out as the work proceeds to prepare for the pointing mortar.

The remaining internal stone walls are to be similarly built of Hollow wa the thickness shewn, and are to be cased with brick-work, the external walls with a space of 4 inches between the brick and stone, the internal walls to have the brick incorporated with the stone.

All these several walls are to be constructed in the best pos- Mortar for sible manner, with good, flat, even bedded stones laid in mortar ble work. compounded of one-third best hard burnt lime from the Gloucester quarries, and two-thirds clean sharp gravel or coarse sand, the interstices of the stone work to be filled with stone chips or spaults, and grouted with lime and sand in a liquid state every foot in height; the mortar to be mixed, ground in a pug mill, and used fresh from day to day.

The architects will however reserve the right of changing the above proportions at their discretion.

Thorough bond-stones to be laid throughout all the walls, at Bond-stone intervals not exceeding 6 feet in length and 2 feet in height; having a bed of not less than 3 superficial feet, and a minimum thickness of 8 inches.

All the cut stone dressings are to be set in putty, the external Setting put pointing to correspond with the specimen referred to.

Quoins in all cases to bed on the Walls at least 9 inches and to Quoins. be in no case less than 15 inches long, and 9 inches wide, to rise in irregular heights and have random back joints.

Bricklayer.

The Contractor may make bricks on any of the "Canal Lands" or upon such "Ordnance Lands" as may not be leased between Ottawa City and Hogsback.

SPECIFICATION.

Bricks and bond.

All the bricks used in the buildings are to be the best quality, hard burnt, free from any defect which may impair their strength and usefulness, and all to be of an uniform size. All the external walls are to be cased inside with brickwork 9 inches in thickness, leaving a space of 4 inches between it and the stone wall, and to be bonded to the stone every fifth course in height and sixth brick in length by brick and flat bedded stones and by galvanized hoop iron stays 1½ inches wide, twenty inches long and one-eighth of an inch thick, turned up one and a half inch at each end, these stays to be built in at intervals of 5 feet in length and one foot in height: the brick work to be built up with the stone walling, care being taken to protect the spaces from being filled with mortar or otherwise. All the internal s one walls are to be cased also with bricks, built with and bonded into the stone work as it advances, but without the iron cramps referred to.

50,000 bricks.

The Contractor will be required to place on the site not less than 50,000 good bricks for each block, within one month from the date of signing the contract or the date of the acceptance of his tender.

Brickwork.

The brickwork in the various floors is indicated by red coloring. All the remaining internal walls forming divisions of rooms, or otherwise, are to be built of brickwork: those on the ground floor, brick and a half, or 13 inches; those on the upper floor single brick, or 9 inches. The bricks to be set in mortar, so that no four courses of brick are to rise more than one inch above the actual thickness of the bricks themselves. All the brickwork to be built in Flemish bond for 13 inch, and in English bond for 9 inch walls, and the mortar to be composed of one-third best burnt lime and two-thirds sharp sand, also mixed in a pug mill, and used fresh from day to day, every course to be fully flushed up

Flushing and grouting.

with mortar, and every fourth course carefully grouted with hot grout as before described.

Arches.

Arches brick and a half thick, to be turned over on the basement where vaults occur, unless where the solid ground remains. Similar arches in every case in vaults, at the heights shewn by the sections, the space between the crown of the arch and the floor over, to be built up with rubble masonry at least two feet high; nine inch arches, groined or otherwise, as shewn, to be turned over to receive the paving of the several entrance Halls. All chimney jambs to be in brickwork, the fire-places being 3 feet wide, 14 inches deep, and 3 feet 3 inches high; an arch over the opening, supported in each case by an iron bar 2 inches by one-half inch, bearing 9 inches on the jambs, and turned up 2 inches at their ends.

Single brick trimmer arches to each fire-place, to receive the hearth slabs. *Trimmer arches.*

Brick and brick and a half discharging arches, respectively to each opening for doors, windows or otherwise, built clear of the lintels. *Dischargin arches.*

Arches to be used in every other case were shewn and necessary.

Build all chimney flues and flues for ventilation or otherwise, also of brickwork, extending to the apex of the roof, or to the point of the roof where it will be connected with the external shaft, which will be of stone, the corbelling over, in cases where it occurs, to be carefully done. All these flues to be pargetted with good adhesive mortar or cement, and all carefully cored at completion of the building. *Chimney f*

Each vault is to be constructed with brickwork of the thickness shewn and figured, and built in the best and strongest manner, the inside casing throughout to be done with Toronto pressed bricks, neatly laid and pointed. In every case, the vaults and Record Rooms are to be cased externally with the best English fire bricks, set in fire clay, one brick or 9 inches in thickness, and bonded or cramped to the stone work, as will be considered necessary by the architects. The walls of the Record Room to be cased inside with Toronto pressed brick, neatly laid and jointed, and left free from plastering at completion. *Vaults.*

All window and door jambs, and arches, and all quoins on the basement are to be brickwork; the window benches also, except otherwise specified, to be paved with bricks on edge, laid in cement. *Window ar door jambs.*

Provide and lay the pugging described in carpenters specification. *Pugging m tar.*

Chases to be left in the walls for soil and water-pipes, and for all purposes of heating and ventilation. The briklayer is to set all grates, and perform every kind of labor required in completing the building, in respect of the various departments of work where his services are required. *Chases for pipes, &c.*

The whole of the drains are to be constructed with the patent earthenware glazed socket pipes, laid with a current, bedded in sand, and set with cement, that description of pipe being used of which half the socket is made to lay on after the pipes are fixed, for facility of access to the drain and removing pipes without breakage. *Drains.*

2

Size of drains and traps.

The principal drains are to be 12 inches diameter, and all subordinates ones six inches diameter, 1000 feet in length of each to be estimated for. All connections to be by branches, either square, oblique or circular, and to be trapped at every proper point, viz : at connection with rain-water pipes, soil pipes from water closets, surface water drains, and where else may be considered necessary. These drains to be carefully cleaned inside as they are fixed. All turns in the drains to be made by easy curves, using circular pipes for the purpose : no abrupt turn to be made in any case.

Cut Stone Mason.

Kind of stone.

All the stone used for dressings of the buildings is to be sand-stone, from Cleveland, in the State of Ohio, Malone stone, in the State of New-York, or other approved quarries, to be carefully selected, sound, and free from all stains or other blemish, and to be protected during the progress of the buildings, so that at completion, all mouldings and projections may be perfect and complete. The whole of the sand stone dressings, including Plinths, Window and Door Jambs, Heads and Mullions, Tracery, String Courses, Eaves Course, Finials, Buttress Caps and Slopes, Parapets, Chimney Shafts, Caps and Mouldings, and otherwise, on the external fronts, are to be wrought, moulded, and set according to the drawings and details at large, now prepared, and which will be prepared from time to time during the progress of the building, the present drawings giving a fair specimen of the general character of the whole work. All copings on parapets and other portions where the upper surface of the stone is exposed to the weather, are to be both set and joggled in hydraulic cement. The carving of stone, including Shields, Coats of Arms, Bosses, and otherwise, is to be done by first class workmen, who are thoroughly initiated into their business.

Carving.

No carver will be allowed to work except under the sanction and licence of the Architects.

Coats-of-Arms.

The principal entrance to be surmounted by the Royal Arms, carved in stone in relief, size, 4 feet square, and a similar shield, having the Canadian Arms, in the principal Tower.

Steps.

Solid stone steps, built on rough masonry, and fenced with an iron railing, to be fixed in the position shewn, leading from the basement to the ground level. The gallery in principal tower to be formed of slabs of Malone stone 5 inches thick, built into the walls, moulded, joggled, and dowelled, as will be directed.

The entrance door steps are to be bush hammered work in limestone of the district, as before referred to, and set in such a manner as will hereafter be directed by the Architects. Each step to be in a single stone. Steps bush hammered.

All the rooms of the basement, except otherwise described, are to be laid with stone paving on a substratum of 6 inches of dry rubble. Stone paving.

Coping 6 inches thick, weathered and throated, are to be laid over the walls, having a projection of 3 inches on each side, dowelled and joggled at the joints. Copings to areas.

Perform all labour required in cutting and setting the sandstone dressing, in joggling, dowelling, cramping, and otherwise working it as may be ordered from time to time by the Architects, till the completion of the buildings. Cramping.

Perform also all labour required in cutting holes for pipes of various kind, or in cutting corbels, bearings for timber, or in any other way required by the various artificers in carrying out the several departments of the contract. Jobbing.

Provide and fix in each room having a fire-place, a chimney-piece of Arnprior marble, made according to drawings which will hereafter be provided by the Architects. The patterns may be varied to suit the rooms,—those in the Governor General's Departments and in the rooms occupied by Chiefs of Departments and the Deputy Chiefs, to be of the prime cost value of 36 dollars. The remaining rooms to have chimney-pieces of the value of 24 dollars. Chimney-pieces.

Each fire-place to have also an approved potsdam sandstone hearth slab, size 4 feet 6 inches long, 1 foot 9 inches wide, and 3 inches thick, set in mortar on the brick trimmer arches. Inner hearths to be also of the same material. Hearth-stones.

Chimney pieces on the basements to be of plain stone, with hearth as before described. Basement chimney-pieces.

All stone cutters and carvers work must be executed at the works unless by special permission to the contrary which the Architects will only grant in very exceptional or urgent cases, and certainly not at all in relation to carving. Stone cut on the works.

The external arches of the v ows and doors to be formed as shewn on the drawings, with sandstone, in two varieties of colours, the red stone from Malone being used in contrast with the lighter stone. Relieving arches.

Each of the Entrance Hall floors terminating at the inner doors, is to be formed of a bed of concrete 9 inches in thickness, and upon that a layer of finer concrete 1½ inch thick formed of Hall and basement floors.

2 *

gravel about the size of a pea and clean sharp sand and hydraulic lime, and on this a layer of Portland cement 1½ inch thick mixed with a proper proportion of fine sand, this finishing coat to be laid by the Plasterer. This cement is to be laid in the best and most workmanlike manner and as will hereafter be directed, and so floated that no joint or unevenness may be seen after completion. The concrete to be formed of the best well burnt hydraulic lime (fresh burnt) mixed in the proportion of one part of lime to seven parts of gravel sand and broken stones. The lime is to be ground under the edge runners and left dry under cover in bags till required for use. The paving of the basement rooms and passages to be formed with the same material.

Entrance porch.
The entrance porch is to be constructed with sandstone as before specified, the piers, arches, frieze, cornice, &c., being in large blocks, cramped and dowelled together in the strongest manner ; the ceiling to be groined in stone built over with rough masonry, and covered with stone slabs worked and set according to the drawings.

Tower groining.
The ceiling also of the principal Entrance Tower to be groined in stone carefully built on centres and fixed in the strongest and most approved manner, and to be built over with rough masonry as will be directed.

Vaults paving.
The vaults to be paved with sandstone from Malone, State of New York. or other approved quarry, in slabs 4 inches thick.

Stone door jambs.
The door jambs and heads of the vaults, in every case, to be of solid stones strongly cramped and dowelled together, secured to the brickwork by iron stays, and rebated to receive the iron doors, the frames of which are to be built in as the work advances, or framed so as to be bolted through the entire thickness of the jambs which will be determined hereafter ; the steps in each case of Malone sandstone or other approved quarry, to be solid and to have the jambs built on their ends.

Quoins for girders.
The quoin of the wall which will receive the iron girders supporting the small Tower, is to be built of solid blocks of sandstone dowelled together, set in cement, and cramped to the rough walling, in such manner as will be directed by the Architects.

Stone templates for girders.
Solid stone templates 1 foot 6 inches thick, 3 feet long, and the full width of the wall, to be placed to receive the ends of each iron girder throughout the buildings.

Ashlar casing in tower.
The walls of the large tower up to the groining to be cased with 6 inch ashlar properly bonded and secured by iron cramps to the rough walling.

All dowels used throughout the buildings are to be of Slate 1 Dowels. inch square and 2 inches long.

Carpenter.

All the timber used throughout these buildings is to be of the Kind of lumber. best marketable quality, free from sap, shakes, large loose knots, or any other defect which can be considered to impair its strength and usefulness. All timber used for joiners' work to be unexceptionable, and the whole to be thoroughly dry and well seasoned by time. Kiln dried timber will not be allowed to be used. Lintels averaging 5 inches thick to be used over all openings for doors or windows, for fixing joiners' work, to have 6 inch bearing in the walls, and of the full width of the wall in every case.

Each of the buildings is to be enclosed by a close fence, at the Clerks of works' offices. contractors' expense, so that all access to the works may be prevented excepting by permission. He is also to provide offices for the Clerk of Works, all sheds necessary for the preparation of stone work, joiners' fittings, and otherwise, and all suitable sheds for the proper protection of lumber and the various description of artificers' work or fittings. All the timber required for internal fittings, and all the flooring board that will be required, is to be deposited on the ground within three months from the date of the signing of the contract, to ensure its being properly seasoned. (This precaution will be strictly enforced.)

Centres to be used in the construction of all arches, securely Centres. fixed, and not struck without the consent of the Architects.

Provide and fix all Wood bricks which may be directed, and Wood bricks necessary for securing the joiners fittings, and all bond timbers and bond. for floors and roofs.

Those portions of the ground floors of both buildings which are Ground floor not paved, and not excavated for cellar,—are to be laid with joists. sleepers and joists of cedar, the joists being first hewed on the upper surface to receive the flooring, and having at the smallest end a diameter of 9 inches after being hewed. Fix sleepers to receive the joists, hewed on the upper and under surface, 7 inches thick, to be laid on dwarf walls at distances not exceeding 9 feet apart. The joists to be hewed at the ends and bearing on the sleepers, and placed at a distance of 2 feet from centre to centre, the bearing on the walls 1 foot at each end.

The whole area to be laid on with 2 inch grooved and tongued Flooring boards. thoroughly clear flooring boards, the width in no case exceeding 6 inches, and not less than 4 inches ; and the boards in each separate room or passage of an uniform width, side nailed with 3½ inch nails; all heading joints made on the middle of the joist, and carefully fixed. All the flooring boards throughout the building are to be laid after the skirtings are fixed and made to fit tightly thereto.

Upper floors. The remaining portion of the ground floor, all the upper floors, and ffoors to the third stories, excepting record rooms and vaults, are to have joists of pine timber 12 inches by 3 inches, placed at distances 16 inches from centre to centre, every fifth joist 13 inches deep, to receive the ceiling joists, all laid with a bearing of 9 inches on the wall at each end, and the whole, including cedars of the ground floor, are to be placed lengthwise of the building in the rooms and crosswise in the passages, allowing the flooring boards to lay the longest way of the rooms or passages.

Cross strutting. All these joists to be carefully trussed with cross struts, at distances not exceeding six feet apart, and the whole surface of these floors, and wherever joists are used, is to be pugged with 2 inches of mortar mixed with chopped hay, and laid on with a guage, pugging mortar to be provided and laid by the bricklayer, the false flooring to receive the mortar, being cleft each piece not exceeding 4 inches in width and 1½ inch thick; an inch iron bolt with heads and screws to be passed through the middle of the joists secured at the ends, and drawn up to a curve to support the floor. The whole area to be laid with flooring boards similar to that described for the ground floors.

Pugging boards.

Iron bolts.

Tower floors. Similar joists and flooring the various towers and in the large tower, forming a room between the vaulted ceiling and the reservoir above.

Trimming joists. In every case of fire-places and flues the joists are to be trimmed, or to rest on corbels, and all trimmers to be 4 inches thick, 4 inches mitered borders to all hearths.

Floors in roofs. Fix throughout the roof in each building tiers of joists extending the whole length of the several corridors, and bearing on the walls 9 inches at each end. Size of joists 10 x 2½, laid 20 inches from centre to centre. Bond timber to receive the joists in all cases 4 x 2½; the walls built level with the top of the joists. Lay on throughout these passages flooring board 1½ inch thick grooved and tongued, and fixed as directed for the other floors.

Railing in roofs. Fix also throughout these passages on each side a strong fence supported on pillars 4 inches diameter placed at intervals of 5 feet, upper rail rounded 4 x 2½, two intermediate rails 5 x 2.

Tanks. Fix in each of the towers a reservoir for water in the position shown on the section. Those for the smaller tower to be formed of a frame of timbers 14 x 10, supported on strong stone corbels

and placed 4 feet wide from the wall all round, the open space
being in the middle of the room ; a space to be left in each case
for access to the rooms. The intermediate joists 12 x 3, properly
framed and floored over as the other portions on the third or attic
floor ; the tank itself to be formed by making a strong king post
truss of the several beams 4 feet high and filling in the sides with
studs and a head to form the tank, 1¼ iron bolt for the trusses.
The inside lining of the tank to be with two inch grooved and
tongued boards ; the outer casing 1½ inch of the same description.

Every precaution must be taken and provision made for pro-
tecting the various cisterns throughout each building from frost.

The reservoir in the large tower to be constructed with timbers Large tank.
16 x 12, framed and trussed with queen posts in the strongest
possible manner, resting on corbels, and having intermediate
joists for the flooring, framed and bolted as before described, to be
4 feet wide and 4 feet high, clear size, braced and secured in such
a manner as will hereafter be directed. Similar inside and outer
casings as described for the other tanks. Each tank to be floored
over, and to have a man hole provided for access thereto.

Roofs.

The roof of each building to be constructed with framed Queen- Roof scant-
post couples, placed at distances not exceeding 10 feet apart, rest- ling.
ing on templates let into the wall, having purlins, pole plates,
wall plates, rafters, collar beams, &c., according to the sections
and details at large, and of the following sizes : Tie Beams, carefully scarfed, 12 x 8 ; Couples, 12 x 6 ; Queen-posts, 12 x 8 ; Collar
Beams, 12 x 8 ; Joists of flat, 10 x 3, placed 14 inches from centre
to centre ; Struts, 8 x 8 ; Outer Joists to receive rafters, 10 x 5 ;
all the joists to be securely braced and strutted ;—Pole Plates,
9 x 5 ; Purlins, 9 x 5 ; Wall Plates, 9 x 4 ; Rafters, 5 x 2½, 14
inches from centre to centre, securely notched on and spiked to
the principal timbers ; Hips and Valleys, 10 x 4, secured to
strongly-framed angle ties. The roofs to be covered with 1½ inch Roof boarding.
sound white pine or hemlock boards, no boards wider than 9 inches
laid close, and all of an even width throughout their length, and
every joint broken ; also to have strips to receive the slates, size
2 x 1, nailed to each rafter with 2¼ inch nails. The flat to be
laid with 1½ inch grooved and tongued boards, to receive the gravel covering, and laid to a current towards each side, a roll to be
fixed at each side of the roof, and the felt neatly dressed over on
the slating. The whole surface of the flats of the main roofs to
be covered with felt, and laid on with tar and gravel, in the most

approved manner, the gravel to be carefully washed before being used, and mixed with a portion of clean sharp sand.

Rooms in roof. The rooms in the roof to be constructed as shewn on the plans, and fitted in every particular as those on the lower floors.

Ceiling joists. Ceiling joists to these rooms, 5 x 2 ; ceiling joists to the lower rooms throughout 3 x 2.

Iron bolts. The couple to be secured by $1\frac{1}{2}$ iron bolts at the queen-posts, and iron straps $2 \times \frac{3}{4}$, to the principal rafters, and the whole to be subject to the direction of the Architects during the progress of fixing.

Tower roofs. The roofs of the various Towers to be constructed as shewn by the sections, the hips let into strong angle ties. Strongly framed couples also to support the roofs on flats, directions for which and detailed drawings will hereafter be given. The minor buildings, water closets, and photograph rooms, to be covered with flat roofs as described for the main building, laid to a current, and prepared for lead ; the photograph room prepared for skylight. It is to be distinctly understood that the whole of the roofs are to be made perfect with all necessary struts, ties, trimmers, templates, fillets, tilting pieces, &c., and with all necessary bolts and straps of iron and also all proper gusset pieces gablets, deckings &c., having the same size rafters, pitching pieces, plates and boarding as the adjoining roofs.

Quarter partition. A framed and trussed quarter partition to be placed on the upper floor, forming the water closet, &c. between the Governor General's and aide-de-camps' rooms ; size of principal timbers 6 x 4 ; studs 6 x 2, to be cased on each side with inch grooved board and filled in with saw dust or tan bark, carefully secured from leakage.

Doors. All the outer doors are to be framed according to the drawings and details at large ; and together both the frames are to be of wood thoroughly dry and well seasoned ; doors three inches thick ; frames, rebated, 6 x 6, firmly fixed to the stone jambs, the doors to have large iron octagonal-headed nails on the outer sides, as shewn. Doors to be hung by strong wrought iron hinges, prepared to a given pattern, and secured by inside bolts and strong dead lock, with suitable inside and outside furniture bronzed. Framed, pannelled and moulded inside jamb linings to match, and architraves inside, the soffits and architraves framed to the same curve as the head of the door frames. (See drawings at large for details of these doors).

Inside doors. All the inside doors to be of pine, framed in six pannels, moulded and chamfered. Size of each, 8 feet high by 3 feet 2 inches wide and 2¼ inches thick finished. All these doors to be hung to framed, pannelled, and moulded 2 inch jambs to match, rebated on each edge, and finished with moulded architraves, according to the detailed drawing, a block to be fixed in each case in the wall to receive the screws of the hinges. Each door to be hung with three 5 inch butt hinges and furnished with 6 inch mortise lock. The door furniture to be of the best quality, subject to the approval of the Architects, the locks to be of English manufacture, and of the prime cost value of 3 dollars. Double doors in every case leading to water closets.

Doors in the basements to be strongly framed and pannelled 2 inches thick, size 6 feet 9 inches x 3 feet, hung to solid rebated frames by 4 inch butt hinges, and furnished with best 6 inch Carpenter's rim locks; plain linings and soffits to all door-ways, finished with a beaded edge; the outer doors to be furnished with a dead lock and 2 inside bolts. **Basement doors.**

All the windows to be framed and fitted, as shewn on the elevations, with transom rail, central pillar, and sashes 2½ inch finished thickness; sashes in every case made to slide through the soffit, which is to be framed for the purpose. Boxed frames prepared, and solid double sunk and weathered oak sills. Those windows which have mullions are to be cased inside with a framed and pannelled facing as shewn. (See detail drawings.) **Windows.**

Framed and pannelled and moulded side linings, soffits, backs and elbows, in every case, and architrave to correspond with those to the doors, 7 inches wide, moulded to pattern. **Linings.**

Each window to be hung with Patent sash lines, brass axle pullies, cast iron weights, and to have the best brass sash fasteners. **Window fittings.**

Each window also to be prepared for and fitted with a second or winter sash, made to correspond with the principal ones similarly hung and fixed, and having suitable fastenings for winter use—made to slide up in the summer months. **Winter sashes.**

Those portions of the various windows above transoms or in tracery, are to be single thickness, permanently fixed. **Fixed sashes.**

The staircase windows and windows of the towers, are to be made to hang with lines and pullies, direction for which will be given. **Staircase windows.**

Suitable casements and fittings to be placed on the several positions where borrowed light is required, and shewn on the plans. **Borrowed lights.**

Casements 2 inches thick, with solid rebated frames 4 x 4, having oak sills, are to be fixed throughout for windows of the basement, **Basement windows.**

hung with butt hinges, and having suitable fastenings, plain linings of deal 1 inch thick to the jambs and soffits, and for window benches, finished with a bead on the edge similar to the doors.

Dormer windows. Fit up dormer windows in the roof where shewn, and according to detail drawings which will be hereafter prepared. Fit up also on the photographing room a suitable window and frame, with all the necessary provisions for carrying on the art of photography.

Telegraph offices. Fit up a room in the attic of each building, with the necessary arrangements for a telegraph office.

Water closets. Fit up the various water closet lobbies with 2 inch grooved and tongued divisions, 2 inch 4 pannelled door in solid rebated frames fitted with 4 inch hinges, 4 inch latch, and inside bolt; the partition to be 7 feet high, with a neat capping on the top. Each closet to be fitted with framed seat riser and cover, on suitable bearers, made to remove and fix readily, the fittings to be of oak or other hard wood.

Cisterns. Provide and fix also in each lobby a cistern for urinal, as shewn on the plan, enclosed in a pannelled and moulded frame, with doors and shelf underneath, the door fitted with hinges and small cupboard lock. The washing troughs to be enclosed in a similar manner.

Basement closets. The closets of the basement to have plain deal seats and risers fixed on strong bearers, plain framed ledged doors in rebated frames 4 x 4, fitted with latch and inside bolt.

Staircases.

Staircases. Each set of staircases to be fitted up as shewn on the plans, having steps and risers, balusters and rails, strings, &c., all of oak of best quality, perfectly dry and well seasoned. Steps and risers grooved together and glue blocked, housed into 3 inch wall, and outer strings, moulded on the edge, and intersecting with the skirtings of the corridors; steps 2 inches thick; risers $1\frac{1}{4}$ inch.

Balusters. The balusters to be 3 inches diameter, turned and moulded and twisted.

Handrails. Moulded handrail prepared in oak, size 7 x 5.

Newels. Newel posts of oak prepared from 8 x 8 timber, the first newel at foot of the stairs being 10 x 10, wrought, moulded, fitted and carved, as will be shewn by future drawings.

The Newel of the principal staircase to be more elaborately finished.

Screws. Provide a sufficient number of hand-rail screws and other iron supports, for completely fixing the staircases.

Carriage pieces. Fix also strong and suitable carriage-pieces to receive the stairs.

All these staircases to be pannelled underneath with 1½ inch Soffits of stairs.
moulded and chamfered oak framing. The landings on each to
be carefully framed; and the boards glue jointed.

Two sets of these staircases—one in each building—to be con- Attic staircases.
tinued through to the attic floor.

Steps also to be fixed in the attics, leading to the various rooms Trap doors.
in the towers, where required, with hand-rails, balusters, string-
boards, &c., complete. Traps to be provided in the roof of each
tower, and in three suitable positions on each building for access
to the flats. These traps to be secured by bolts inside.

The carpenter is to provide all labor required in laying in the Casing and job-
various pipes for heating, fixing gratings, and otherwise, for ven- bing.
tilation, and in making all the preparations for laying on the gas,
casing-pipes, or otherwise; he is also to furnish such labor and
material as may be necessary to enable the various artificers to
carry on and complete their several departments of work.

Plasterer.

The mortar for plastering of the first and second coats to be Mortar.
compounded of the best hard burnt lime of the district and
clean sharp gravel or coarse river sand, mixed in the proportion
of 3 parts of sand and 2 parts of lime, and a sufficient quantity of
long cow hair. The lime to be all run through a screen, and
mixed at least 3 months before it is required to be used.

The lime used for the finishing coat of plastering is to be White finish.
brought from Guelph, mixed with fine sharp clean sand.

All the laths used in plastering are to be cleft instead of sawn, Laths.
sound and hearty, well seasoned, and in every respect perfect.
Sappy or knotty laths will in no case be allowed in the buildings.
The joints to be properly broken every 12th lath and all large
timbers are to be counter lathed so as to form a proper key for
the plastering, all nailed on with the best lath nails of the weight
of 5 lbs. to the 1000.

All the walls and ceilings throughout the buildings forming Plastering.
rooms, passages, halls, and otherwise, excepting only the roof, are
to be respectively lathed, rendered, floated and set; the finishing
coat white. The whole of the work to be executed in the best
possible manner, floated perfectly true, and trowelled to a hard
and smooth surface.

All angles and arrises to be wrought true and plumb. Angles.

Cornices with one enrichment to be fixed to the ceilings of the Cornices.
principal or Governor's entrance hall and staircase and Governor's
apartments, girth 24 inches.

Cornices also with one enrichment, to be fixed to each other entrance hall and staircase, to each room used by the chiefs of departments, and the deputy chiefs.

Cornices without enrichment throughout the various corridors on both floors and the remaining offices. The average girth of these cornices 20 inches, made to such drawings as will hereafter be provided by the Architects.

Bracketing, &c. The whole to be backed out by chips of brick or stone set in plaster, or bracketed with wood, as will be considered necessary.

Skirtings. The skirtings to be all formed with cement of some approved quality, a specimen of which is to be prepared and submitted to the approval of the Architects. They are to extend down to the joists and laid on previously to laying the flooring, backed out with chips of brick or stone, projecting $1\frac{1}{4}$ inch from the finished plastering, moulded and worked to a smooth and even surface. Average girth of skirtings 12 inches, more or less, in various rooms, as may be determined on. Those on the basement rooms to be plain, 6 inches high, with 1 inch projection.

Cement floors. All the floors mentioned in cut stone Masons Specification are to be of Portland cement, done as there directed. The cement to be the best Portland cement manufactured by Messrs. B. White & Co., Milbank, London, England, and the Contractor will be required to produce and deliver to the Architects a written guarantee from the manufacturers that their best cement has been supplied. The cement is to be mixed with an equal quantity of clean sharp washed river sand laid to the proper thickness and finished all in one coat, the greatest care to be taken in joining the work where left off at any time, and when possible the entire surface of the floor is to be finished off by sufficient hands so as to shew no joint; where joints have to be made the work must be cut back to a strait edge as will be directed, and the fresh work connected with it by the smallest possible joint; all joints where made are to be parallel.

Repairs. The whole of the plastering is to be left in a sound and perfect state at completion of the buildings, any repairs being made which may be rendered necessary during the progress of the various departments of work.

Keenes or Martin's cement. All external angles of chimney breasts, or otherwise, to be worked in Keenes' or Martin's cement made perfectly straight and plumb.

Archways. The several archways in the corridors to be constructed as shewn, chamfered on the edges, all worked by trammels and made perfectly true.

All the rooms on the basements which are not plastered toge- Lime white.
ther with the water closets and offices, are to have two coats of
white lime wash, the brick or stone work being first neatly pointed
with mortar.

Slater.

All the roofs are to be covered with best Duchess slates, partly Kind of slates.
from the Eastern Townships, and partly from Vermont, laid on
in the manner shown by the roofs on the elevations, partly dia-
gonally. They are to have 3 inches bond, and nailed with $1\frac{3}{4}$
inch strong copper nails, 2 in each slate.

Hips and valleys cut straight and true, the slates to finish Cutting.
under a felt roll at the ridge, and a lead roll at the hips. Double
courses at the eaves and ridges.

The slates are all to be perfectly sound, free from blemish of Left perfect.
any kind, and the whole to be of an uniform color, left in a perfect manner and without any broken slates at the completion of
the buildings.

Plumber and Iron-Founder.

All the plumber's work is to be done with milled lead of the Milled lead.
best quality.—

The several Water Tanks in the Towers to be carefully lined Tanks.
with lead 6 lbs. to the foot, the smaller cisterns supplying the
water closets, with lead 5 lbs. to the foot,—all properly fixed and
soldered at the joints.

Fix to the valleys also 5 lbs. lead 20 inches wide, dressed over Valleys.
a fillet on each side, and allowing 6 inches fully between the
edges of the slate.

The Hip rolls and ridges to be covered with lead 6 lbs. to the Hips.
foot, 20 inches wide, dressed neatly on to the slates.

Provide and fix also to all chimneys, down the sides of all Steps and
towers, side walls, or otherwise, which extend above the roofs, 5 flushings.
lbs. lead, stepped flushings cut in one piece, and averaging 18
inches wide carefully secured to the stone work by wedges, and
pointed with cement.

Lead flashings also to be used in all cases when necessary, and
as will be directed by the Architects.

Cover the flats of the towers, water closets and photographing Tower and
room with 6 lbs. lead laid on rolls where required, and dressed flats.
over in the most approved manner.

Closet apparatus. Fit up the water closets each with a best pan closet apparatus with blue basin, sunk handle, and all the necessary cranks, and wires, &c., complete.

Trap. Provide and fix to each a 4½ inch strap, and 3 feet in length of 4½ inch lead soil pipe, 6 lbs. to the foot, soldered at the joints and connections with the trap. The remaining portion of the soil pipes extending to the drains to be 6 inch cast iron pipes, the connection between it and the lead to be tinned and soldered. The connection between the trap and closet pan to be in the usual manner with red lead, cement, &c.

Rising main. The main supply for the water tanks to be by 2 inch middle sized lead pipe, carried immediately under the ground floor joists, and running up the towers in a chase formed in the wall, each tank to be furnished with an 1¾ inch ball tap, to shut off the supply, and a 3 inch iron waste pipe, connected with the drain.

Supply to closets. The supply to the water closet cisterns to be by 1 inch middle sized lead pipes, also furnished with an inch ball cock, and a 2 inch iron waste pipe.

Supply to Lavatories. A ¾ inch supply pipe to the pans of the closets; ¾ supply pipe also to the urinals—the flow of water through these to be constant during the day, and made to shut off at night.

A ¾ inch supply pipe also to the washing troughs, each fitted with plated cocks, waste washer, plug and chain.

Waste pipes. 1½ inch waste pipes of lead, each trapped and fixed to the several urinals, and each washing basin. All these waste pipes to connect with the main soil pipe of the water closets; each trap to have a screw washer at the bend, for the purpose of cleaning out, if required.

Iron pipes. The quantity of supply pipes for the water tanks to be reckoned from its entrance to each building nearest the engine; all pipes used outside the building to be of iron, and to form a separate contract after the plan of general supply is determined.

Hydrants. Provide and fix in such portions of the building as will be hereafter determined on, 6 brass hydrants, 3 inches in diameter, for attaching the hose to in case of fire, or for other required uses; these to be connected with the main supply pipes, to the tanks, and six 2 inch brass stop cocks in connection therewith.

Quality of iron. All iron work used in the buildings is to be the best quality of wrought or cast iron, properly prepared for its various uses.

Fire-proofing. Provide and fix to the floor over the record rooms rolled iron joists, 7 inches deep, I shape, and of the usual thickness, placed 14 inches apart, and bearing 6 inches at each end on the walls; the space between to be filled with galvanized iron wire netting, to receive the pugging between the joists, and the plastering of the ceiling below. The whole area to be pugged with mortar 4 inches thick—suitable provision to be made in these joists to receive the flooring board of the room above.

Provide and fix to each vault and record rooms 2 framed iron Iron doors. doors, the outer one prepared on the best principle, double sheeted with wrought iron plate, securely rivetted to the frame. The inner door to be of a lighter description, sheeted only on one side each to be hung with strong wrought hinges, and furnished with best locks.

The frames to be prepared of wrought iron, $1\frac{1}{2}$ inch square, with Iron door uprights, head and cell strongly put together, and built with frames. stone work, or with iron, 3 inches x $\frac{3}{4}$ inch, both for the inner and outer frame, fixed in a rebate in the stone jambs and bolted through their entire thickness with 1 inch bolts.

For each set of iron doors and frames, locks for the outer doors, Cost of doors. and fastening for the inner ones, the sum of two hundred dollars may be allowed as the prime cost, exclusive of fixing.

Provide and fix also to in the record room and vaults one thou- Iron shelves. sand feet in length of perforated cast-iron, shelves, with divisions and standards complete.

Provide and fix also to each record room and vaults which have Iron shutters. windows, one set of framed iron shutters, securely hung to iron frames built inside the walls, and having proper inside bar fastening.

The eaves of the roofs throughout to be supplied with cast-iron Eaves gutter. gutters, made to the drawing at large; the casting to be made so that the joints shall be fair outside, the stone made level to receive the gutter, which is also to be secured to the wall plates. The joints made water tight by proper iron cement.

Fix in the several positions shewn on the roof plan, twenty pipes Down pipes. for conveying off the rain water, 6 inches by $4\frac{1}{2}$, cast square, or in any other shape which may be determined on hereafter, and according to drawings to be prepared; and to terminate near the ground with a shoe, throwing the water outwards into the surface drains. All angles of the gutters to be cast solid, at least one foot long on each side.

Ornamental cistern hands to each rain water pipe. Hands.

Provide and fix also in each water closet lobby a cast iron Urinals. enamelled urinal trough, of the size and description shewn in the plans.

Lavatories. Provide and fix also in the same apartments a cast iron enamelled washing trough, with two basins in each, as referred to in the plumber's department.

Iron girders. Cast iron girders to be fixed to support the small tower in the west end of the left hand block, and also to support the wall over the photograph room. These girders may be estimated to contain 200 lbs. weight to every foot in length.—Detailed drawings and directions relating thereto will be provided hereafter by the Architects.

Tarring iron. These girders to be tarred over when hot, and painted previously to being fixed in the wall.

Iron cresting. The roofs to be provided with a crest work of wrought iron, made to an approved design, and fixed all round the outer edges of the flat,—care to be taken in fixing to prevent leakage through the felt covering. This work may be estimated at $3 per foot, running measure, prime cost, exclusive of fixing.

Iron terminals. Provide also wrought iron work for the termination of the various towers, as shewn on the drawings, and as will be more fully described by detail drawings, to be prepared hereafter. The sum of $1200 dollars may be allowed as the prime cost of these various works, exclusive of fixing.

Iron bolts and brackets. Provide also all iron staps and bolts for the roof, for the tanks, for floors, fixing the eaves gutters, for all internal fittings staircases and otherwise, all locks, hinges and bolts, all window fastenings, stay bars, and bars for fire-places, all pipes for water supply, both hot and cold, all iron railings for staircases and gallery in tower, together with the ornamental gothic brackets, iron railing, also to the external areas and basement steps, and every other description of iron work required in the building, and in carrying out the various departments of the work, even though not specifically mentioned.

Register grates. Provide and fix in the several fire-places throughout both buildings register grates of the average prime cost value of $24 dollars each, exclusive of fixing.

Ventilators. Provide also, and fix in each room valvular registers for ventilation, fixed in the most suitable situations which will be hereafter determined on. $8 each set to be allowed as the prime cost value of these.

Spiral staircase. Fit up in the large tower a cast iron spiral staircase, with pierced treads and riser, extending from the floor over the groined arch to the floor above, to be 5 feet in diameter, and carefully fixed.

Heating. The heating and gas fittings are not included in this contract, but will be specially provided for by separate tender, hereafter.

Fix throughout all the walls, both of stone and brick, at the level immediately under the window sills, 2 rows of 5 tiers each, in stone walls, and 3 tiers in brick walls, of 1½ inch patent hoop iron bond, rivetted at all joints and cross walls, and resting on an even surface prepared for the purpose, passing through all openings of doors or otherwise, and not cut out until ordered by the Architects. *Hoop iron bond.*

The whole to be heated and covered with tar, and sanded, previously to being laid on the walls. The two tiers to be laid on the wall at an interval apart of six inches in height. *Coating bond.*

Glazier.

All the windows, except those described below, are to be fitted with best 32 oz. British sheet glass, when the square does not exceed 5 feet superficial. Above that size 42 oz. glass is to be used, laid in putty, bradded and back puttied. The outer or winter sashes to be similarly glazed with German sheet glass. *British sheet.* The windows of the various staircases, entrance halls, and those terminating with the corridors, are to have colored glass of such design as will hereafter be given. 75 cents per foot may be taken as the prime cost value of the glass. The windows in the water closet, and other closets having borrowed light, are to be glazed with plain, obscured glass of a given design, value 50 cents per foot, prime cost. *Colored glass.*

Painter.

All the wood and iron work usually painted, and not otherwise described, is to be carefully knotted, stopped and primed, and to have three additional coats of plain oil painting, of such colour as will be determined on hereafter. All external iron work also to be painted in 4 coats of oil, plain colours. *Four coats oils.*

The iron crests on the roofs to be picked out in various colors, as will be directed. *Picked colors.*

All window frames and sashes to be painted externally in plain colors. All internal doors and windows of the ground and first floor, and attics, with their fittings, to be stained with 2 coats of Asphaltum, of an approved patent, and twice varnished. All the oak fittings, whether doors, linings or otherwise, handrails, newels, steps and balusters of the staircases, are to have two coats of best copal varnish. *Staining.*

Cement skirtings to be painted 3 coats in plain oil colors, grained to match the fittings of the rooms, and once varnished. *Paint on cement.*

3

SPECIFICATION

Of additional works to be done in making Fire-proof the two Departmental Buildings at Ottawa, C. W., according to the accompanying Drawing and Memorandum attached.

~~~~~~~~~~~~~~~~~~~~~~

Omit the timber joists as originally specified, and substitute in lieu thereof, for the ground and first floors of each building and the 3 attic rooms of right hand block, rolled iron joists on Fox & Barrett's Patent; they are to be placed 20 inches from centre to centre, throughout both floors of each building, and to bear 9 inches at each end on the walls resting on a course of proper stone templates throughout. The size of joists to be regulated according to the length of bearing by the memorandum attached to the drawing, and are to be thoroughly coated with paint or tar previously to their leaving the mill. *Rolled iron joists.*

Lay throughout the floors fillets of deal about 1½ inches square, resting on the flanges of the iron joists, placed nearly closed together to receive the pugging, these strips to be cleft on the upper surface and edges and sawn only on the under side. *Fillets.*

Provide also and fix underneath said strips, ceiling joists of pine 2 x 1½ inches to receive the laths of the ceiling, placed 12 inches from centre to centre. *Ceiling fillets.*

Provide also, and lay in the concrete fillets of pine 2½ inches square and 16 inches apart, to receive the flooring boards; these fillets to be secured by struts or otherwise, as will be required and directed by the Architects. *Flooring fillets.*

The flooring of the several rooms and corridors to be completed according to the original specification. *Flooring.*

The ceilings also to be as originally specified with cornices, &c., complete. *Ceilings.*

The whole area of the floors to be laid with concrete 9 inches thick, composed of best hard burnt lime and gravel or cracked stones, in the proportion of one part lime, five parts coarse gravel or broken stones and bricks and one part fine gravel, and clean sharp sand, the whole thoroughly incorporated together, mixed with water to the proper consistency and placed on the fillets to a regular guage in two layers of about 4½ inches each, the first layer being allowed to harden previously to laying on the second, and each to be carefully trodden or rammed together. *Fire-proof concrete.*

3 *

The coarse gravel or broken stones to be passed through a screen of one inch gauge, and the finer gravel through a screen of half an inch gauge and no stones to be of a larger size.

Lime.

The lime to be of the very best quality, fresh burnt for use from time to time, as required.

The gravel carefully prepared, free from pebbles and deleterious matter of any kind, and mixed with a portion of clean sharp sand, as will be directed.

Large iron joist.

Iron joists of larger size prepared to a given pattern are to be placed as girders to the staircases, and in any other situation where they may be required to receive the ends of intermediate joists, and also for trimmers to fire-places.

Easings.

Provide and fix all necessary easings and mouldings to said trimmers as previously specified.

Staircases.

Each staircase to be constructed with solid Ohio or other approved stone, spandrel steps of the sizes before specified for the oak stairs. They are to be built into the walls, one foot at the ends and each step joggle pointed.

Landings.

Landings in every case 6 inches thick, in one stone, the whole to be carefully cleaned off to an even surface on the under side, having raking soffit, and left complete in every respect.

Handrails and newels.

The Contractor in preparing his estimate for the foregoing works will omit the staircases, as specified, excepting only the hand rails and newels which will remain as before.

Balusters.

The balusters throughout are to be of wrought iron of such design as will hereafter be determined on, yolted to the stone and secured in the best manner to the hand rail, the sum of five dollars may be estimated as the prime cost per yard of the balustrade throughout, exclusive of fixing.

The basement staircases to be also of stone with plain iron bar balusters and flat round iron hand rail, yolted to the stone steps, and fixed in the best manner.

Conditions.

This specification is to be incorporated with, and to form a part of the original specification for the whole buildings, subject in every respect to all its clauses and conditions, precisely as though it had been originally included therewith.

SCHEDULE

Of fixed Rates and Prices for Labor and Material, supplied on the ground, and required in the erection of the New Departmental Buildings, City of Ottawa, forming the basis of the accompanying Estimate and Tender. The scale of Rates here following to be allowed in valuing work for progress estimates, as well for alterations, additions or works dispensed with, together with Extras, to be measured and calculated solely by the Architects or Clerk of the Works in charge, from time to time.

———

To WIT:

	$ Cts.
In earth, clay, or gravel, per cubic yard	0 21
In rock, do do	0 52

Fire clay pipes with cemented joints,
4 inch, 14cts , 6 inch, 23cts., 9 inch, 35cts., 12 inch, 42cts.,
    15 inch, 52cts., diameter per foot run.
4 inch, 13cts., 6 inch, 22cts., 9 inch, 34cts., 12 inch 41cts.,
    15 inch, 51cts., laid dry, per foot run.

Brick barrel drain in mortar, 12 & 18 inch diameter, per foot run	0 45

Arnprior marble, unwrought, delivered, per cubic foot..	1 05
Ottawa lime stone, do do do do ..	0 21
Ohio sandstone, do do do do ..	0 45
Caen Freestone, do do do do ..	0 70
English firebrick, unlaid. do per 1000	35 00
Ohio or Malone stone pavement flagging, per foot super..	0 25
Vermont and Eastern Townships slating laid with copper nails in the best manner, per square	6 65
Minton's Eucaustic tiles, in plain colors, laid in the best manner, per foot super	0 77
Marble paving, white and black checkers, in the best manner, per foot super	0 60

Rubble stone masonry in lime mortar, in foundations, per cubic yard	1 58
do do in Cement do per cubic yard	2 19

	$ Cts.
Rubble stone masonry in mortar above ground level, per cubic yard	1 75
Random coursed work do do do per cubic yard	2 53
Coursed masonry, hammer dressed, per cubic yard	3 64
6 inch ashler, per foot super	0 30
Rough bouchard face, per foot superficial, stone included.	0 35
Fine bonchard face, do do do do ..	0 38
Chisseled or tooled face, per foot surper., plain surfaces, stone included	0 42
Rubbed do do do do ..	0 44
do for moulded work do do do ..	0 53
Concrete laid, per cubic yard	2 45
Interior walls for plastering, laid in mortar, per M 20 bricks reckoned to the foot, per 1000	6 30
Exterior walls, chimnies, &c., laid in mortar, per 1000.	7 00
Brick work in arches, laid in mortar, do ..	6 65
Brick paving on edge, laid in mortar or sand, do ..	8 75
Brick nigging laid in mortar, per 20 bricks to the foot..	7 00
White or red pine, rough or unframed, for beams, plates, girders, brestsumers, &c., per cubic foot	0 15
Cedars 12 in diameter, per foot, lineal	0 12
Pine floor Joisting, B. M., per M	0 16
Studding or quartering, B, M., per M	0 17
Rafters, pulins, &c., B.M., do	0 19
Bond timbers, wall plates, &c., B. M., per M	0 16
Trussed partitions, per square	4 90
Herringbone strutting, per hundred feet run	7 00
Pugging, per square, 3 inch thick, sound board included.	1 75
Battering walls, &c., per square	1 40
Centreing per square foot	0 07
Bracketing for cornices and projections, per foot, surper.	0 10

	THICKNESS.		
	2	1½	1
	$ cts.	$ cts.	$ cts.
First quality pine battens, laid per square	5 90	3 85	3 15
do do oak do do.	7 70	5 25	4 20
Second do pine do do.	4 55	3 50	2 80
do do oak do do.	6 65	4 55	3 65

$ Cts.

	THICKNESS.	
	$1\frac{1}{2}$	$1\frac{1}{4}$
	$ cts.	$ cts.
Pine roofing boards, grooved and tongued laid per square....................	2 45	2 10

Clear seasoned lumber best quality, B. M., per M...... 13 30
Common inch boards, B. M., per M..................... 8 40
Oak in scantling, planks or boards, unfixed, per M, B.M. 25 20
Casings to beams, jamblinings, &c., dressed and fixed,
    per lineal foot.................................. 0 35
Staff and angle beads, fixed........................ 0 05
9 inch single faced moulded skirtings fixed, per foot run. 0 14
12 inch double faced   do   do   do .. 0 21
16 inch   do   do   do   do .. 0 28
do do in Keenes or Martins cement................ 0 18

2 inch four pannelled moulded framed doors, of pine 30cts,
    and oak 35cts. per foot super.
2 inch six pannelled moulded framed doors, of pine 35cts.
    and oak 40cts., per foot super.
Six inch single faced moulded door and window archi-
    traves, per foot lineal........................... 0 08
Eight inch double faced moulded door and window archi-
    traves, per foot lineal........................... 0 17
Ovolo rising sashes, double hinge, with all requisite
    frames, weights, pullies and fastenings, per foot super. 0 35
Ovolo french casements, hinged and fixed, per foot super. 0 25

Lath, plaster, float and set, per yard super........... 0 21
Render, float and set   do   do 0 18
Guaged work in ceilings, coves, &c., per yard super.... 0 24
Plaster cornices, per foot girth..................... 0 14
Centre flowers fixed, per foot diameter............... 2 80
Lime White basement walls, per yard............... 0 03

Milled Lead Laid, per cwt........................... 7 00
Zinc Covering, per pound.......................... 0 14
I. C. Tin Roof Covering, per square................. 10 50
Best Charcoal IX Covering, per square.............. 12 00

	$ Cts.
Galvanized Iron Gutter, per pound	0 17
Ornamental Iron Work, per pound	0 17
Cast Iron Girders, per pound	0 03
Wrought Iron Straps, Bolts, &c., per pound	0 12
Cast Iron, per cwt	3 10
Cast Iron Gutters and Pipes, per cwt	3 50
Felt, Tar and Gravel on roofs, per square	4 20
In white lead, oil, knotting, stopping and priming	0 05
Two coat work, per square yard	0 04
Three do do	0 07
Four do do	0 09
Add for graining and twice varnishing, per square yard.	0 28
Distemper or ceiling and walls, do do	0 07
Staining in Patent Asphaltum Stain, do do	0 09
Smethwick English Sheet, per foot super	0 35
Best English Crown, do	0 45
Seconds do do	0 38
Best German Sheet	0 14
Ornamental or colored glass, 10 per cent allowed over cost	0 00
Gothic lozenge glazing in metal frames, per foot super..	0 21
Carpenter's wages, per day	1 25
Joiner's do do	1 25
Bricklayer's do do	1 50
Stone Mason's do do	1 25
Stone Cutter's do do	1 60
Plasterer's do do	1 50
Labourer's do do	1 00
Slater's do do	1 50
Stone Carver's do do	2 50
Wood Carver's do do	2 50
Painter's & Glazier's do do	1 25
Plumber's do do	2 00
Tinner's do do	1 50
Blacksmith's do do	1 25

All works not enumerated to be valued by the Architects, at fair current rates.

STENT & LAVER, Architects.

Ottawa, October, 1859.

INDEX.

4